THE WITNESS

WRITTEN BY
ROBERT WESTALL

ILLUSTRATED BY
SOPHY WILLIAMS

First published 1994 by Macmillan Children's Books,
an imprint of Macmillan Publishers Limited,
a division of Macmillan Limited,
25 Eccleston Place, London SW1W 9NF,
and Basingstoke.
Associated companies throughout the world.

This revised edition published 1995.

ISBN 0 333 63789 5

9 8 7 6 5 4 3 2

A CIP catalogue for this book is available
from the British Library.

Printed in Hong Kong.

A great wind blew out of Asia; from that finger of ice that would one day be called Everest. It thundered across white Steppes, and disturbed the King of Parthia's slumbers. Cyrenius, Governor of Syria, tossed and turned, worrying about the Egyptian furniture, shipped to Rome three days before.

Across the desert the wind blew icy and dry. But when it reached the warmth of Jordan it dropped flurries of snow. One of them caught the cat as she reached the crest of the stable roof. She crouched wretched; the wind blowing her fur into wild saucers, exposing points of warm, pink, vulnerable skin. She spat into the wind's face in helpless fury.

Her misery was total. She was heavy with kitten. In this, her first year of exile, she was unprepared for the Judean cold. Worse, she couldn't find a dark private place to give birth. Turned out of cellar and byre by servants putting down straw and blankets for extra guests. Strangers everywhere.

Egypt had been so different: basking in the sun on the temple terrace; dabbling for fish in the green waters of the temple canal; the manicured hands of the priests, who thought it a prayer to stroke her. The common people would hold back the carts while she stepped past. In Egypt, she was a goddess, the spirit of Bastet-Ra, Mother of the Sacred Trinity, cat-goddess of Bubastis by the Nile. Parents would sell the hair of their children to bring her offerings, watch with bated breath as she washed, counting the number of times her paw crossed her ear, believing that this foretold the future.

This stable was her last hope. Leaking roof, flaking mud walls that let in draughts, old straw full of the smells of other animals. But better than nothing. If she gave birth in the open, the wind would kill the kittens before morning.

She leapt to the ground, with a sickening grunt. Yet even in her wretchedness she was graceful. Golden, long-legged, huge-eared.

In the doorway, she spat again. People even here; poor people too, from the smell. Rich strangers were sometimes well enough. Their perfumes reminded her of the temple. They might stroke her, feed her from their own rich food bowls; but poor people drove her out with shouts and blows . . .

She still couldn't understand why her world had changed. One morning she had been lured from the temple by the breeze from the quayside. Lost in a dream of fish, she had met a bearded stranger in the alley. She had paused, one foot uplifted, waiting for him to step aside. Instead, rough hands seized her and thrust her into the sudden darkness of a sack. Such outrage! Then such endless blind jogging! Such sickness, such hunger, thirst and the unbearable smell of her own filth! Such useless gnawing and clawing to escape!

Finally, rough guttural voices and the chink of coins.

"Sure she's good at killing rats?"

"Good? She's the reason there's always corn in Egypt. Have you never seen the Egyptians' granaries? How d'you think they keep rats out? These creatures are such ratters the Egyptians worship them."

The other man made a noise of disgust, deep in his throat.

"You are asking me to take a devil of Gehenna into my house!"

"Better a devil than rats, brother. The price of this particular devil is still seven denarii. If the Egyptians had found her in my baggage they would have slain me."

Her sack was rudely thrust into ruder hands. The neck was pulled open, and she was tipped on to a mud floor so hard it hurt her paws. Then a door slammed and she was in the dark again. She sat down and washed her shoulder to calm herself. Suddenly a rustling among the straw made her ears prick. At least she would not go hungry.

When she had killed and fed, she found a hole in the wall and rapidly enlarged it. Outside, in an utterly strange blurred landscape, and a thousand smells, all alien, she crouched to relieve herself. She was free; but all roads were the same, and none gave even a whiff of Bubastis, no matter how much she widened her nostrils to the breeze. From that day, her prison became her safe place and hunting ground. Her new owner, picking over the remains of her kills, was well enough pleased, and ignored her.

Others were less kind. When she descended to the ground men cursed and kicked her, and children threw stones; so she learned to keep to the rooftops and the night. But when the weight grew in her belly, and the flurry of kicking inside warned her that the time had come to find a safer place still, she knew she must not stay in that barn . . .

She had turned away from the stable door when an even crueller blast of wind caught her, at the same time as the first contraction in her belly. Making the bitterest of choices, she turned again, and slipped inside. It was dark, but to her eyes clear as crystal. Near the door a plough-ox chewed the cud lazily, lying half on its side. The straw where it lay was thick and clean, but no good for a nest. The creature might roll, crushing mother and kitten altogether in the moment of birth . . .

Further in a grey donkey stamped. A striped blanket had been thrown over its back, and a man fussed around it with furrowed brow and a cross, anxious voice. His breath and the donkey's steamed together in the frosty air. Further in still, a woman lay, on straw not so thick and clean as the ox's bed. A lamp gave her light, and enough warmth to hold her hands out to. And there was a patch of shadow in the corner behind. The cat crept forward, silently, sagging belly pressed close to the floor.

But the man saw her, shouted. Reached for a long stick. He blocked her retreat. She leapt into the shadowed corner, back arched and teeth bared. The man advanced, but the woman put up her hand.

"Nay. Have mercy. She is in the same plight as myself. Are we so poor we can't share what we have?"

"Dirty things . . . if the child should be born tonight . . . they lie on children's faces and steal their breath . . ."

"Nay. She will soon have enough to keep her busy. And see, she is clean. She is the cleanest thing in this poor place." The man turned, spreading his hands.

"I'm sorry! I *always* stay with my father's cousin when I come here. He must have known I was coming for the census. So why is his house full of strangers? I will tell you why. Because strangers have money. It is the Romans' fault; they destroy the old ways . . ."

"Husband, husband. Calm yourself. You are not to blame for your father's cousin. I shall do well enough here." The man grunted, soothed.

"But let the little cat stay. She will keep me company. All women find this waiting dreary.

See, she's snuggling in."

And, certainly, the cat's fear seemed quite gone. She crouched against the woman's robe, kneading furiously with her forepaws.

The cat could not understand it. She could still feel the draughts catching at her fur, yet she was deliciously warm. The spiky straw seemed as soft as a silken temple cushion. And though the lamp guttered, the room seemed bathed in golden light, brighter than the sun on the temple of Bastet-Ra. She slowly crept up the robe, till her nose rested against the woman's neck. But the woman formed a nest in the straw of the dark corner, and put the cat into it; and there presently two kittens were born. Two only, for the winter-gods had been merciful. She purred with pleasure at having company during the birth; in the temple at such times, she-cats were never left alone . . . Licked dry, the kittens began to purr also; tiny bee-like buzzings. And thus, contented, they must all have slept.

For when the she-cat wakened, there had been a great change. Even the big animals, in their stupidity, were aware of it, let alone a god-cat. The lazy ox had lumbered to its feet and was staring, drooling in shining strands right down to its straw. The donkey had stopped wheezing and stood quite still. Both were intent on a feeding-trough in which lay a man-kitten.

But an even greater change had taken place. Glowing winged figures stood silent all around. They were as tall as trees. Yet they all stood within the small stable. The cat, quite outfaced, sat up also, and licked her shoulder to soothe her nerves. Then, greatly daring, she walked across to the first great figure and, one paw raised enquiringly, sniffed it. The scent of the creature was overpoweringly beautiful; better even than the lotus-flower in summer. She went on to the next, and the next. Each smelt differently, but all Heavenly.

Among the winged figures came a ripple of mirth.

"The cat sees us. Even the ox and ass. Why cannot the man?"

For the man was walking up and down, frowning thunderously.

"Are you sure you're all right? Is the child well? I would be happier if the midwife came to look at you . . ." He walked straight through one of the great winged figures. The cat, watching, arched her back in alarm. But nothing happened, except another ripple of mirth among the winged creatures.

"Husband, we have no need of a midwife. It was an easy birth. How could it have been otherwise?"

The man grunted, deep in his throat. "Oh, I know, I know."

"Cannot you even feel those who guard us? The little cat can *see* them!"

Just then, the Child opened His eyes. The golden light that had been in the stable was as nothing to that which was suddenly there. The glowing beings covered their faces with their wings. But the she-cat inched towards him, as if drawn by a magnet.

"Look out, Mary, the cat!"

But the furry body stopped short, feet folded beneath her and green eyes blinking as she might have blinked at a fire. And such a storm of purring as threatened to shake her apart. The woman said, "Let her worship also."

The cat dozed again, till the door banged back and the frosty wind blew in. Five men stood there, in greasy sheepskins. Their eyes seemed to fill their faces, and their mouths were permanently open. Having shut the door, they shuffled uneasily.

"This be un place. See, there's babe in feeding-trough. And more o'they bright-shining fellers. Beggin' yer pardon, gaffer." They all bobbed to the nearest winged creature.

The woman's husband came forward.

"What are you jabbering about? You can't come in here. We're packed out already."

"But the shining feller spoke to us. Told us we were to come, and what we'd find. And here it be, just like he said . . ."

And without another word, they knelt to the Child. The cat shifted uneasily but held her station, even when the newborn lamb bleated loudly, leapt from a shepherd's arms, and ran straight into the oil lamp, nearly setting the straw alight. Stupid creature, thought the cat. But then lambs were not reared in temples . . .

The shepherds left in the end, persuaded to take their noisy lamb.

"It needs its mother," said the woman.

The Child slept again, and the great light dimmed, but did not depart. The man sat in the doorway, as if on guard, but soon he pulled his robe up around his ears, his head dropped, and he slept the racking, snoring sleep of exhaustion.

The woman closed her eyes, but did not sleep. The smile stayed on her face, even when she eased her aching body on the straw. The cat lay, desiring never to move from this place again.

But in the far corner, something rustled in the straw. The cat's ears pricked. She turned.

A rat was coming towards the Child. It moved slowly on its belly, as if dazed. Its little red eyes shone.

Outrage filled the cat. The worst thing in her world was approaching the best. She wriggled her lean bottom and pounced. The rat squealed once as she bit into its neck. The man and woman came to, with a start.

Then they saw what had happened.

"See, she guards the Child," said the woman sleepily.

"They have their uses," grudged the man, and dozed again.

The taste of rat's blood in her mouth made the cat feel ravenous.

But, far more important, she now had a gift to bring the man-kitten. She crept nearer, dragging the limp body. The Child opened His blue eyes, and the cat laid the rat by Him.

But there was no praise or pleasure for her. The Child's grief over the rat broke over her like a storm, till she hunched her body, laid back her ears, and whimpered in pain.

The Child tossed restlessly, flung out one tiny arm towards the rat. The creature's poor death-flattened belly gave one frantic heave, its eyes opened and shone red and bright. Slowly it dragged itself to its feet and inspected itself with a bewildered twitching nose.

Then side by side, cat and rat watched, until the cock crowed.

By the time the rich men came, the kittens had their ears half-pricked and their eyes wide open, and they were driving the she-cat frantic with their wobble-legged journeys through the straw. When the Child heard them draw near, He would give a gurgle of delight. The kittens were well-fed, sleek like their mother. But not with the killing of rats, not ever. There was no need; now there were always scraps in plenty.

When the rich men had presented their gifts, and were sitting at ease with the mother, they noticed the cat.

"So the star has led others here before us?"

"How so?" asked the woman.

"Even the gods of Egypt come to worship. This is a sacred cat from Bubastis' temple on the Nile. When did they bring her? She is a gift greater than ours."

"She arrived on her own, in the very hour of the Child's birth."

"Incredible," said Melchior.

"Unbelievable," said Caspar.

"Egypt knows the stars," said fierce-moustached Balthasar.

"What manner of god is this Bastet-Ra?" asked the woman, curious. "Does she demand blood-sacrifice?"

"Nay," said Melchior. "She is a gentle god, a country-people's god. She brings fertile harvests. Maidens pray to her for a husband, and married women for an easy childbirth. Her worship is through dances and merriment and the right mothering of children. Egypt is a kindly place, under her rule."

"She is a demon," said Joseph. Recent events had mellowed him a little, but not much.

"Nay, husband, be not so narrow. Good is always good. These good men are not of our ways either, but they have come so far to be here. Tell me, Melchior, of the place this little one came from."

So Melchior spoke of the broad-bosomed Nile, and the yearly flood that brought fat crops, so that none starved. And the people going down the river to Bubastis, singing and dancing on the brown-winged ships.

"Poor little one," said the woman, stroking the cat's fur. "How you must miss the sun."

The rich men had gone. They had talked of Herod; and when they talked of Herod, they lowered the lids of their shrewd eyes, and shook their heads. Something worried their subtle minds. When they left, they didn't go back to Jerusalem, though that would have been their easiest way.

There was always peace in the stable; but less than usual that night. The man tossed and groaned in his sleep. Suddenly, he awakened with a frightened shout.

"What ails you, husband?"

"I have seen an angel of the Lord."

"Thanks be to God he has taken away your blindness."

"You do not understand. It was the Dark Angel: the Angel of Death."

Clinging together, they turned to look at the sleeping Child.

"What are we to do? Were you not told?"

The man laughed harshly.

"I was told to do one thing, that I should have done days ago. I was told to take that devil back to its owner." He threw a stick at the cat, which missed. The cat withdrew into a corner, calling the kittens to her urgently.

"But we do not know the owner . . ."

"*I* do – I have asked around. Aaron bar Joshua. A godless man who bought her from a Syrian camel driver . . ."

"But how will that help us?"

The man gave a laugh as short as a curse.

"The angel forgot to mention that."

The woman said thoughtfully, "Aaron bar Joshua is *not* the owner. He bought her from a thief. Her real owner dwells in the land of Egypt . . ."

"Woman, we cannot go to Egypt. How would we live? They are expecting us back at Nazareth. We have tarried *here* too long . . ."

"Would you disobey an angel, Joseph? Even *that* angel?"

In spite of the great danger, there was a last ripple of mirth among the great winged figures; their light was dimmer, now, but the cat could still sense them.

"We shall take this little one home," said the woman, in a voice that was low but determined. "And we shall make a home there ourselves, until another angel comes."

And so, next morning, they packed hastily. And Joseph's father's
cousin, repenting of his coldness (and having heard some talk of kings,
gifts and a Messiah) found he could lend them all manner of things,
including a second donkey. And so they went from Bethlehem more
comfortably than they had come. And on the second donkey's back, twin
kitten-heads poked from among the baggage.

And as each dawn turned the sky pink over the distant lands of Egypt, a swift long-legged streak ran before them, across the flat plains of Sinai.

The cat of Bastet-Ra was going home.